February 16, 1860, isn't a date I'm likely to forget. Besides being my twelfth birthday, it was the first time I'd ever laid eyes on a dead man.

When the dying man whispers the whereabouts of the mysterious Massacree Mine to Jeb's pa, it's the first step in a riproaring Western adventure. Refusing to believe that he's an orphan after Pa disappears, Jeb teams up with balloon-borne quack Dr. J. Augustus Weatherby, and together they head into Nevada territory. . . .

Will Jeb and his companion reach the Massacree Mine and uncover its secret? Will they survive the vicious Washoe zephyr and the deadly Apache bonnet? Will they escape the double-crossing desperadoes in time to save Jeb's pa from the hangman's noose? There's comedy and action galore in this wild and woolly tale of suspense, treachery, and treasure.

ORPHAN JEB AT THE MASSACREE

by Stephen Mooser

pictures by Joyce Audy dos Santos

Alfred A. Knopf
NEW YORK

This is a Borzoi Book Published by Alfred A. Knopf, Inc.

Published in the United States by
Alfred A. Knopf, Inc., New York, and simultaneously
in Canada by Random House of Canada Limited, Toronto.
Distributed by Random House, Inc., New York.
Book design by Mimi Harrison
Manufactured in the United States of America
1   3   5   7   9   0   8   6   4   2

Library of Congress Cataloging in Publication Data
Mooser, Stephen.   Orphan Jeb at the Massacree.
Summary: Jeb, twelve years old in 1860, sets out alone
for Nevada in search of his long-absent prospector father,
only to be told he is in jail about to be hanged for murder.
[1. West (U.S.)—Fiction. 2. Robbers and outlaws—Fiction.
3. Buried treasure—Fiction] I. Dos Santos, Joyce Audy, ill. II. Title.
PZ7.M788170r 1983   [Fic.]   83-99
ISBN 0-394-85731-3   ISBN 0-394-95731-8 (lib. bdg.)

This book is for
Sid Fleischman

Contents

ORPHAN JEB
AT THE
MASSACREE

Chapter One

THE DEAD MAN

February 16, 1860, isn't a date I'm likely to forget. Besides being my twelfth birthday, it was the first time I'd ever laid eyes on a dead man. That's not to say people hadn't died while I was growing up in Placerville. A few years earlier, when gold fever had hit Northern California, Placerville had been just about the roughest place on earth. Hardly a week would go by without someone croaking in a mine accident or getting plugged in a fight down at the saloon. It happened all the time. I just never seemed to be around for the show.

But those days were gone now, just like the gold that used to fill the hills. And most of the miners were gone, too, having drifted off to better pickings. My pa, though, he'd stayed. He scratched out a living panning streams, all the while keeping an eye out for that big nugget that was going to make us rich. He liked to joke that his goal was to get rich quick—even if it took him a hundred years! And sometimes it seemed like it would. He was always going off adventuring after the latest big strike and coming back with empty pockets.

I didn't like it when Pa left. Ma had died when I was born, and so whenever he went away, he'd put me up with the Pritchetts, the Reverend and his wife, Sarah. They were kindly enough, but about as humorless and hard-driving as you can get.

On the day we saw the dead man, we'd been into town for our weekly shopping. Pa had picked up a package at the leathersmith's shop. He wasn't saying what it was, but I was hoping it was a birthday gift.

Pa had promised to buy me a steak supper at the Lazy Dog Café, but the sky had suddenly filled with clouds, and there was a taste of rain in the air.

"Jebediah," said Pa, "I think we'd best be getting home. Those clouds look ready to spit, and I already had my bath this week. Let's ride."

Our only horse, an old mare named Cyclone, was waiting where we'd left her outside the café. We mounted up double and set out for our cabin in the hills above town. Before long, drops of rain began raising puffs of dust along the road. Pa urged Cyclone on, but she kept to her usual pace, which was somewhere between slow and stop.

We were plodding along this way when we suddenly came upon the scene of a terrible accident. A red buckboard, its sides splintered, was lying upside down in a ditch just off the road. The horse was still attached to the reins, and the poor creature was raising a terrible fuss trying to break free.

"Jebidiah, jump down," yelled Pa. "Help me cut loose that horse."

It wasn't until we loosed the horse that we found someone trapped beneath the overturned wagon. A man's arm and a leg were sticking out from under the broken rig. Pa took hold of the arm and checked for a pulse.

"He's alive, but barely," he said. "Grab hold. Let's see if we can't raise this wagon up enough to drag him free."

The rain was steady now, and the pine needles lining the ditch were slicker than grease. I planted my feet as best I could and heaved. The wagon shuddered.

"Again!" cried Pa. Again we heaved with all our strength, and the wagon lifted. Pa slid a rock beneath the rig to keep it off the man, and then we pulled him free.

He looked half dead. There was blood on his face and coat. After a while, his eyes fluttered open. He tried to speak, but no sound came out. Pa bent over and put his ear close to the man's mouth. He listened for a moment and then raised up and said, "Jebediah, take Cyclone and hightail it back to town. Round up Doc Tombs and hurry him out here."

"Yes, sir," I said. I took a last look at the stranger, climbed out of the ditch, and leaped to the saddle.

By now the rain was pouring down in great silver sheets. I lowered my head into the storm and made for town. We had gone less than a hundred yards when Cyclone suddenly stopped. I looked up to see two riders blocking the way. One was a monstrously fat man with long, stringy hair that had been matted to his face by the rain. The other man was a bug-eyed fellow in a derby hat.

He shouted to me above the downpour. "Have you seen a red buckboard pass this way?"

"Not pass by," I called back, "but there's a rig like that just over the hill. The driver's been hurt. I'm on my way to fetch a doctor."

The two exchanged worried glances.

"That driver would be our brother," said the fat man. "We'd appreciate you showing us where he is."

"He's hurt mortal bad," I said. "I'll have to get the doctor first."

"You can save yourself a trip," said the fat man. "Festus here is a doctor."

A doctor! I couldn't believe my good fortune. And perhaps the stranger's too.

"Follow me!" I said.

Chapter Two

MASSACREE MILLIONS?

We were back at the buckboard in no time. Pa was still bent over the stranger.

"Pa!" I shouted. "I found a doctor!" Pa looked up and the man named Festus tipped his hat.

"There may not be anything you can do, Doc," Pa said. "I believe he's just passed on."

The two appeared thunderstruck at the news. They scrambled off their horses and practically fell over each other getting to the buckboard.

Festus poked around the stranger's body, looking for signs of life. When he had found none, he sadly announced, "Sorry, Bart, he's croaked."

Fat Bart sat down heavily at the base of a pine and buried his head in his hands.

Pa turned to Festus. "My name's Jake Harper," he said. "And this here's my boy, Jebidiah. The departed said his name was Orville Means. He a friend of yours?"

"More than a friend," said Festus solemnly. "He

8

was our brother. I'm Festus Means, and the man over there is Bart Means."

Pa gave Festus a dubious look. "That's strange," he said. "Mr. Means didn't mention any relatives in these parts."

"A man that's been headstruck often can't recall his own name," said Festus. "Orville's got a heap of kin. Besides us, he's got a mother over at Grizzly Flats. It's her birthday tomorrow, and we were heading for the celebration. Looks like we'll be holding a funeral instead."

"You have my sympathy," said Pa.

"I'd like to have more than that," said Bart, rising to his feet. "If you don't mind, I'd like to know what my brother's last words were."

Pa paused and scratched his chin. "All he said was that his wheel had snapped and the buckboard had flipped. The rest was just mumblings."

Bart took a step toward Pa. "Go on, go on, what kind of mumblings? Did he mention anything about Nevada or a place called the Massacree Mine? Think hard now. I'd be comforted if you could recall his final thoughts."

Pa shook his head slowly. "I can't say I heard him speak of the Massacree Mine."

"Blast!" stormed Bart. "Confound that old coot. It's just like him to up and die."

With a great deal of grunting and groaning, Bart picked up the dead man and hoisted him over his shoulder. "Come along, Festus. We'd best be getting

Orville home." Then he turned to Pa. He narrowed his eyes and asked once more, "You sure he didn't say anything about the Massacree?"

"As the doctor said, he was headstruck. He could barely talk," said Pa.

The fat man dumped the body over the back of his horse. Then he and Festus mounted up and trotted off.

After they had left, Pa said, "Come on. Let's get out of here."

I was more than happy to go. The dead man had given me an uneasy feeling inside, and so had the two live ones.

When we got to the cabin, our clothes were soaked and our boots thick with mud. Muddy boots would mean extra work for me that night. Cleaning them was my job, but I didn't mind doing it because Pa's boots were something special. Everyone said they were the finest pieces of walking leather in California. And they were fancy, too. On the outside of each boot the leathersmith had stitched a big red *H*. The *H* stood for our name—Harper. Pa was proud of those boots and so was I.

We changed into dry clothes. Pa lit up the fire in the big stove, and I got out the rags and polish.

"Hand me your boots, Pa," I said. But instead of his boots, Pa gave me the package he'd picked up in town.

"Happy birthday, son," he said. "Go on, open it up."

I tore into the wrappings. There was a box inside,

and when I opened the lid, I very nearly fell off my chair. It was a pair of boots. Fancy boots, with big red H's stitched into the sides. They were just like my father's.

I looked up to say thanks, but I'd been struck speechless.

"Now everyone will know you're a Harper," he said. "Try 'em on."

They slipped on as smoothly as if they'd been butter-greased.

"I don't believe I'll ever take them off," I said.

That night we sat and polished together.

"I feel sorry for Mr. Means's mother," I said, dabbing a lump of polish onto the toe of my boot. "She won't have much of a birthday."

"I wouldn't worry about that," said my father. "Orville told me all his kin were back in Boston. Those two men weren't his brothers, Jebidiah. They were thieves."

"Thieves?" I said. "What would they want from Mr. Means?"

"They thought he was carrying a map," said Pa. "In fact, I wager those boys are still pawing through his clothes trying to scare it up."

I dipped my cloth in the polish. "What kind of map?" I asked.

"A treasure map, and worth a fortune, Jebidiah."

"Was it a map to that Massacree Mine the fat one— Bart—was talking about?" I asked.

"Yep, but they won't find it on Orville," said Pa with a grin.

I flashed Pa a knowing smile and polished harder. "He gave it to you, right?"

"Not exactly," said Pa. "You see, there never was a map. Orville carried all the details in his head."

I was worried till Pa added, "Now they're all in my head."

"Then you can find the mine," I said excitedly. "Pa, are we going to be rich?"

"Most likely," said Pa. Then he laughed. "Rich enough, at least, to replace those trousers you just ruined."

I looked down at my leg. I felt my face go red. I had been polishing my britches!

Chapter Three
ORPHAN JEB

When I awoke, the storm had been swept away, and the sky was as bright as new glass. I found Pa out front, saddling Cyclone. I didn't have to ask where he was bound. The smell of gold was in the air, and I could almost see his nose twitching.

"You'll be spending the next few weeks with the Pritchetts," he said. "I've got business in Nevada."

"You could take me along," I said.

"Maybe when you're older," he said.

I had a terrible hankering to go after those Massacree millions—and twelve seemed plenty old to me—but no matter how much I begged, Pa wouldn't let me come. By that afternoon, I found myself deposited into the hands of the Reverend Pritchett and his plump wife, Sarah.

"We'll take good care of him, Jake," said the Reverend.

What they meant was that I'd take good care of their church. The Pritchetts were nice enough, but they worked me like a plow horse. I hoped Pa would not be gone long.

Before he left, Pa bent down and whispered in my ear, "Now, if anyone asks, you just tell them I'm off prospecting for silver. Don't mention the Massacree Mine."

I knew it wouldn't be hard to convince people that Pa had been struck with silver fever. For the last year, a whole army of folks had been heading over the High Sierras to Nevada. Silver, tons of it, had been discovered near Virginia City, and the rush for riches was on.

"I'll not say a word," I promised.

"Mind the Pritchetts now," he said, swinging onto his horse. "I'll be back before you know it."

He had barely disappeared down the road when I felt a hand clamp onto the back of my neck.

"Step lively now, Jebidiah," said Sarah Pritchett. "The good Lord wants a clean church, and so do the Reverend and I. You'll find a mop and bucket in the shed out back."

In the weeks that followed, I made myself handy around the Pritchetts' church. When I wasn't busy with my chores, I'd sit out on the front steps of the little whitewashed church, polish my boots, and watch for my pa. Any day I expected to see him come galloping up the trail, wearing a top hat and silk suit. Bags of Massacree gold would be dripping off Cyclone, and there would be a diamond pin the size of my fist stuck in his lapel. Then he'd jump down, sweep me up in his arms, and hug me till we both were crying. That was what I hoped.

But two months went by and then three, and he didn't return. From time to time, I'd stop travelers on their way from Virginia City and ask if they'd seen Jake Harper. But none of them had. It wasn't surprising. From what I heard, no one in Nevada went by their real name. I heard tell of a midget named Half-Pint Harper, a murderer and horse thief named Bad Man Harper, and a one-eyed gambler named Jake the Snake. But none of them sounded like my pa.

I didn't want to admit it, but I couldn't deny it. Something had happened to my father.

Then, one afternoon, I happened on Mrs. Pritchett in the church. She was praying and didn't see me come in.

"Please, dear Lord," I heard her pray. "Watch over him in all his days. Let no harm come to our boy, our Orphan Jeb."

Orphan Jeb! Orphan! The words hit me like a kick from a mule. I staggered back and sank into one of the pews. Mrs. Pritchett heard me and turned.

"Jeb!" she said, getting up and hurrying to my side. "I didn't know you were here."

"Why did you call me Orphan Jeb?" I sputtered. "Has something happened to my pa? What have you heard?"

"I've heard nothing," said Mrs. Pritchett. "And that's

16

just it, Jeb. Your pa should have been back before now. Certainly you know that."

I gulped. "Pa's not dead. He'll be back."

"Don't you worry," said Mrs. Pritchett with a smile, putting an arm around my shoulder. "You'll always have a home with us."

"Pa will be back," I repeated.

But he didn't come back, and by early June, everyone in town had taken to calling me Orphan Jeb. It was a name that fit, but I despised it.

Being orphaned into the hands of the Pritchetts wasn't a life I fancied. And so, one evening in June, with a full moon on the rise, I wrapped some apples and bread into my bedroll, slipped a jackknife into my pocket, and headed out of town. Down by the stream I swung onto the eastbound road in the general direction of Nevada. If my pa was still alive, I intended to look him up.

Chapter Four

A MOST AMAZING SIGHT

When I was a few miles from town, I made a bed of pine needles a short distance from the road and went to sleep. When I awoke, the dawn had just begun to stain the eastern horizon. I shined up my boots with a handkerchief and sliced an apple for breakfast. Long before the sun had crested the tall pines, I resumed my travels.

I was worried about being seen by someone from town, and so I decided to take to the woods till I was well clear of Placerville. I picked up a deer trail and followed it into the pines. For the most part it ran parallel to the road, but at times it meandered off and I lost sight of the road altogether.

I had been on this trail for nearly an hour when a sudden shout froze me in my tracks.

"Unhand my ship, you devils!"

At first I thought it was the Reverend Pritchett. But

as the ruckus continued, I realized it was neither the Reverend's voice nor his words.

"Lay away from that balloon, you knot-headed sapsuckers!"

Cautiously I followed the noise. Soon the forest gave way to a grassy meadow. At the far edge of the meadow I saw a most amazing sight. There, wedged tightly between the limbs of two tall pines, was a big red hot-air balloon. A rope ladder dangled from the wicker basket beneath the balloon. Halfway up the ladder was a thin beanpole of a man in a tall silk hat. He looked madder than anything.

"Unhand my balloon!" he blustered, waving a fist at the silent pines. "Let go, or I'll cut you into toothpicks!"

This was the first flying machine I'd seen up close, and she drew me like a magnet. I wandered, wide-eyed, across the meadow till I found myself standing beneath her. The man was in the basket now, a pointy-nosed fellow with a long face. He was tugging on one of the ropes that held the basket to the balloon. I hadn't been there for more than a minute when he glanced down and spotted me.

"Great snakes alive, boy!" he exclaimed. "What are you doing here?"

"I'm sorry if I startled you, sir," I said. "But it looks like you could use some help."

"I'll need more than that to free my ship," he sighed. "I'll need a miracle. Have you ever seen a sorrier sight?"

19

I shook my head sympathetically.

The man came down the rope ladder and tipped his hat. "I appreciate your kind offer," he said. "Allow me to introduce myself. I am Dr. J. Augustus Weatherby, purveyor of the Heavenly Remedy, the greatest cure known to man."

A medicine man, I thought. The West was full of men peddling cures for everything under the sun. Pa said that the medicine was mostly tarantula juice, which was what the miners called whiskey. Enough tarantula juice and anybody would feel good, said Pa.

"And what brings you to these cursed woods, Mr. uhhh . . . ?" he went on.

"Jebidiah, Jebidiah Harper," I said. "I'm on my way to Virginia City, to find my pa."

"Why now, that's a coincidence," said Dr. Weatherby. "The silver metropolis is where I too am bound. You just can't imagine how many sick folks there are in Nevada. I aim to cure 'em all."

I looked up at his wondrous flying machine.

DR. WEATHERBY'S HEAVENLY REMEDY, it said on the side of the balloon. ANYTHING YOU GOT WEATHERBY'S WILL FIX—PRONTO!

It looked as if I was in luck. In Weatherby's balloon I could be in Virginia City as fast as the wind could carry me. I cleared my throat and shuffled my boots in the pine needles.

"You wouldn't be looking for an apprentice?" I asked. "I've never been up in a balloon before, but I'm quick to learn. I'd be a big help, sir."

Weatherby shook his head. "I'm sure you would, but I couldn't abide the extra weight. We'd never make it over the High Sierras."

"I don't weigh much," I said.

"I can see that. Why, you're no bigger than a match," he said. "But it would be one match too many."

For a moment I had felt Virginia City was within my grasp. Now it seemed a million miles away.

"However," said Weatherby. "If you're still willing, I could use some help getting loose."

"I'd be glad to help," I said.

"Good," said Weatherby. "If you could take hold of the ladder and pull the balloon into the meadow, I'll climb back into the basket and guide her out of the branches."

We said good-bye. Then Weatherby climbed into the basket, and I wrapped my hands around the rope ladder.

Slowly, ever so slowly, I walked away from the trees. I had just about pulled the big balloon free when a sudden gust of wind came swirling up. Before I knew what had happened, the balloon jerked free and shot up into the sky. My hands were frozen to the ladder. When I looked down, I was already ten feet off the ground and rising like a fish on a line.

Weatherby peered over the side of the basket and offered some advice: "Hold on!"

We crested the trees and shot away to the east. I glanced down at the sharp tops of the pines and tightened my grip. My knuckles were white, and my face was damp with sweat.

As we drifted along, I fought my way up the swaying ladder. When at last I reached the basket, Weatherby hauled me in. I sat down at once on a pile of bottles and tried to catch my breath and calm my pounding heart.

"Welcome to the Ship of Health," said Dr. Weatherby with a smile. "Looks like you've just signed on as my first mate."

"I'm sorry, sir," I said. "The wind caught me by surprise. You can set me down anytime you want."

"That won't be likely now," he said. "We can't risk another brush with those pines. We'll just have to pray for a good strong wind. With a solid breeze we could make it yet."

I smiled at Dr. Weatherby and took a look around my new home. The basket was about the size of a large round tabletop. Scores of bottles of Weatherby's elixir, as well as tins of meat and crackers, littered the bottom. And above my head hung a large pail from which smoke was rising.

"There's charcoal burning in that pail," explained Weatherby. "Hot air rises. That's what gives us our lift."

I crawled over a pile of bottles and looked over the edge. Far below I could see a carpet of deep green pines stretching away to the horizon in all directions. It was a view that excited and frightened me at the same time. I couldn't decide whether to shut my eyes or keep them open. I was certain we'd fall at any moment and be speared by the pines.

"Well, mate," said Weatherby, putting an arm around my shoulder. "How do you like sailing on the wind?"

"It's a little scary," I said. "But I'm sure I'll get used to it."

"Used to it!" laughed Weatherby. "Before you know it, you'll be loving it."

And indeed, as the day wore on, I found myself beginning to enjoy life among the clouds. In fact, I spent most of the afternoon leaning over the side, marveling at the countryside slipping silently beneath us. We floated over mountains, hills, and meadows. Far below us dusty roads twisted their way through the rocky Sierras. Along the roads an occasional rider would look up and wave a cheerful hello. But none of the travelers was my pa.

Weatherby pulled out a bottle of ink, sat down on the floor of the basket, and began writing out labels for his cure. Between scratchings he kept up a steady stream of chatter. If he wasn't talking about his miracle cure, he was discussing the weather. And if it wasn't the weather or the cure, it was his balloon. I could hardly sneak in a word.

Late in the day I noticed that the mountains were no longer below us. Either we had drifted down or the peaks had shot up. We were heading directly for a wall of granite.

"Dr. Weatherby!" I shouted.

Dr. Weatherby got to his feet slowly and eyed the approaching mountain. The distance was closing fast. The top of the mountain loomed at least a hundred feet above us. Weatherby quickly sized up the situation.

"We could be in trouble," he said.

"I can see that, sir."

"Could be terrible trouble," he added, wetting a finger and holding it up to test the wind.

"What about stoking the fire?" I asked desperately.

"Not enough time," he said calmly.

"Isn't there anything else we can do?" I asked.

"We could lighten the load," he said. "But to do that in a hurry would mean one of us would have to jump."

"But can't we *do* something?" I cried.

"Yes," he said. "Pray."

The balloon drifted closer. Fifty feet, forty feet. Then we were just twenty feet away. The rocks looked like granite spikes, waiting to rip us to pieces. We came so close I thought I could reach out and touch the cliff. I was sure we were goners.

Then, just at that moment, we started to rise. The face of the cliff shot by us as we climbed rapidly into the sky.

"It's a miracle," I said, wiping the sweat from my face.

Weatherby patted me on the back. "Not a miracle, my boy, a thermal," he said. "A warm current of air. Wind can't get through this mountain any more than we can. When the wind hits the cliff, it climbs. Luckily, it decided to take us along. We're fortunate it's a warm day. Heat makes it rise all the faster."

Within a few minutes we had crested the top of the mountain. The warm thermal shot us up an extra hundred feet before we finally leveled off.

Below us the mighty Sierras began to dissolve into rolling, grassy foothills. Far beyond I could see a rugged, reddish desert.

Weatherby slapped me on the back. "By the blazes, my boy, we've made it! Look at that. It's Nevada. She might not be as pretty as California, but she's teeming with sick and diseased people, and that's all that counts with me. Hee-haw, Nevada! Roll out your crippled, haul out your lame, and pull out your money. Here comes Doctor J. Augustus Weatherby!"

Chapter Five

NEVADA

After a while we cleared the foothills and swept into the desert. The pines first gave way to oak and then to scrub and cactus. Only a few low hills broke the endless sea of reddish sands and bare, exposed rock.

"They used to call this the Washoe Territory, but it's Nevada now," said the doctor. "She may look peaceful, but don't let appearances fool you. At any moment a Washoe Zephyr could rear up and knock us back over the mountains into California."

"Washoe Zephyr? What's that?" I asked.

"Just about the trickiest wind that's ever been invented," said Weatherby. "It's a whirlwind with a mean streak. It whirls and kicks and spits dust every which way. It can strip paint from barns, and feathers from chickens. It can stop after a hundred yards, and then again it can sashay for a hundred miles or more. A Washoe Zephyr is terrible trouble, especially if it catches you up in a balloon."

"Are you expecting to meet up with one of these zephyrs soon?" I asked.

"Can't say," said Weatherby. "But in summer the pesky things are more common out here than jackrabbits. Keep your eyes peeled for a cloud of dust. That's sure to be a zephyr, and we'll want to set down before it hits."

"I'll keep an eye out," I promised.

Within an hour the sun had slipped behind the hills and darkness had begun to creep across the desert. Weatherby put a metal plate over the burning charcoal to lower the fire, and the balloon sank to within ten feet of the sands. Then he tossed the rope ladder over the side and said, "Out you go, Jeb. When you touch down, tie the ladder around a rock."

It took a second for his words to sink in.

"Out? You mean down the ladder?"

"That's your job. You are the first mate, aren't you?"

I glanced down uneasily.

"Hurry up now, before we careen into a cactus."

Gingerly I crawled over the side of the basket and took hold of the swaying ladder. As I skittered down the rungs, I was flicked about like a fly on a horse's tail. After what seemed an eternity, I touched down in a spray of sand and rock. I quickly tied the rope ladder to a pitted rock. Weatherby lowered supplies over the sides as the balloon slowly settled toward the ground. Though the hot air was gone, the balloon remained upright, held taut by a web of thin wires within the great red bag.

We built a small fire near the ship.

My own bedroll had been left back in the meadow, but Weatherby loaned me a blanket, which I spread out nearby.

After a dinner of salt pork and crackers, I took off my boots and started to shine them with my handkerchief.

"Nice boots," said Dr. Weatherby.

"They're the best," I said proudly. "See those *H*'s? They stand for *Harper*. My pa has a pair just like 'em."

As the fire died down to blinking coals, we sat and talked. I told Weatherby about myself and how I came to be on the road in search of my pa and the Massacree Mine. Then Weatherby told me about himself.

"I was peddling memory potion in Kansas when I bought my balloon from a bankrupt circus," he said. "The Ship of Health and I have been together since. Before that I did so many things I can't remember them all."

I prodded him to recall a few.

"Well," he said. "I've tried farming, trapping, and logging. And I've been a painter, blacksmith, and inventor. Mostly, though, I've been a peddler. I guess it's the profession that best fits my fast tongue." We both laughed. Then he added, "I've done and seen a lot, Jebidiah, but I've had my regrets, too."

"Regrets?" I asked.

"Never had time for a family," he said. "Moved about too much, I guess. I think I might have liked to settle down."

29

"You may find a home yet," I said.

"Perhaps," he said wistfully. "Maybe someday."

When the fire was gone, we said good night and crawled under our blankets. I lay awake a long time, listening to the doctor's snores and peering up into the sparkling sky. All the talk about family had made me lonely. I missed my pa.

When I awoke, a gentle breeze was blowing off the hills. Weatherby tossed a handful of dust into the air and watched it drift to the ground.

"The wind's a little southerly for my taste," he said. "But in June you can't be too particular. Load up, Jebidiah. We will have breakfast in the air."

I climbed into the basket and began stacking gear. I was about to help boost Weatherby aboard when I spotted a dust cloud on the horizon. My heart leaped to my throat.

"Zephyr!" I yelled. "Coming this way!"

Weatherby shaded his eyes and peered out into the desert.

"Shouldn't we tie off the balloon?" I asked anxiously.

"No need to, Jeb. She ain't a zephyr," he said. "What's stirring up that dust isn't the wind, it's horses—a whole gang of them. Way I see it, that dust belongs either to miners on their way to town to spend money, or to bandits heading over here to steal some."

Bandits! I'd heard that Nevada bad men would just as soon shoot you as look you in the eye. I hoped I'd heard wrong.

30

Chapter Six

THE SKINHEAD GANG

The cloud soon became a herd of dusty cowboys. There must have been ten or twelve of them. They rode up to within twenty feet of us and reined their horses to a halt.

At first glance, there was no telling whether they were good folks or bad. They all could have used a shave and a smile. Two of them, one a flat-nosed squinty man, and the other a bald-headed fellow, slid off their horses and strode over.

"That's quite a flying machine you've got there," said the bald man.

"Only three like her in the whole world," said Weatherby, "and only one like me. I am Dr. J. Augustus Weatherby, purveyor of the Heavenly Remedy, a cure so powerful they've yet to invent the disease it can't fix. Any of your men sick?"

"Sorry, Doc, there ain't an itch or a sneeze among

us. Anyway, we're not here for the cure. We're after the balloon."

"No charge for looking," said Weatherby with a smile.

"We ain't looking, mister," said the bald-headed man, suddenly drawing a pearl-handled pistol. "We're taking."

"Bandits!" I blurted out. My worst fears had been realized.

"We've been called worse," said the squinty-eyed man.

"Scoundrels!" bellowed Weatherby.

"Even worse than that," said the bald man.

"Why, this is monstrous, sir," raged Weatherby. "Who do you think you are?"

"You mean you don't recognize Skinhead Dickerson?" said the squinty bandit. "Why, he's the most notorious desperado in the Washoe Territory. He's a legend."

"As far as I'm concerned, sir, he's nothing but a common thief," said Weatherby.

"We won't be common much longer," said Skinhead. "How many gangs do you know that make their getaways by air? We'll be uncatchable! No posse in the world can outrun a Washoe Zephyr."

"Come on, boss," said Skinhead's squinty partner. "Let's grab that thing and ride."

"Please don't, sir," I begged.

"Boys! Scramble up into that rig and see if you can't cipher how to make it go. We're heading for the roost," said Skinhead.

Now I was starting to get mad. "You can't just take our balloon," I said. "I've got business in Virginia City."

"It'll just have to wait," said Skinhead.

"But my pa's there . . ."

"Pat, Angus, throw some coals on that fire under the bag," he ordered.

I was furious. If he was going to maroon us, by ginger, I'd leave him something to remember me by.

I lashed out at him with my foot. I meant to raise a knot on his shin the size of a muskmelon. But Skinhead stepped aside, grabbed hold of my foot, and spilled me onto the dust. The gang howled with laughter, and I felt my face go as red as the Nevada soil.

Skinhead himself didn't join in. He was staring at my boot.

"Boy, how did you come by this walking leather?"

I glared at him and held my tongue.

"You know anyone else with the same red *H* cut into their boots?"

I was stunned. "My pa," I sputtered. "He's got boots like these. Do you know where he is?"

Skinhead grabbed my hand and jerked me to my feet. "I surely do," he said. "Boys," he added, turning to his gang, "come on over and shake hands with Bad Man Harper's boy."

I was thunderstruck. Bad Man Harper! That couldn't be my pa. But a second later one of the bandits fished a worn poster out of his saddlebag and brought it over. At the top was a drawing of my pa. It wasn't much of a likeness, but it was his face, all right. Underneath the picture were these words:

WANTED!

BAD MAN HARPER

HORSE THIEF, MURDERER,
&
JAIL BUSTER

Can be identified by a tall "H" cut
into the sides of his boots
Should be returned to Sheriff Ed Grady,
Virginia City, Nevada

$500 REWARD · · · DEAD OR ALIVE

Murderer? Horse thief? I couldn't believe my eyes. That was my pa's picture, but he wasn't an outlaw.

"I don't think there is a man in the whole territory my boys and I respect more than Bad Man Harper," said Skinhead. "Your daddy is the only man in history to break out of the Virginia City jail. That place is built like a bank safe. He's slicker'n wet ice, your pa."

"Then my pa is free?" I asked.

"Not exactly," said Skinhead. "He broke out all right, but he didn't stay out. He was captured not long afterward."

"My pa wouldn't have murdered anyone," I said angrily.

"According to the sheriff, he murdered a peddler named Festus Pangborn. Stole his horse, too," said one of the outlaws.

"My pa wouldn't do that," I said. "He must have been framed."

"Lots of folks thought the same," said Skinhead. "Back in March they were all set to let him go for lack of evidence. But then he busted jail, and that changed everything. Everyone in town figured that proved his guilt, so the sheriff has sent for the hangman. Just in time, too."

"In time for what?" I asked.

"For the Fourth of July," he said.

"The Fourth of July?" I echoed.

"Independence Day," said Skinhead. "Nevada's about to join the Union, and Sheriff Grady has his eye on the governorship. He figures if he can put on a big patriotic display, he'll get noticed by the folks in Washington."

"I still don't see what this has to do with my pa," I said.

"Why, he's the main attraction," said Skinhead. "Grady's scheduled a parade and speeches in the morning, fireworks in the evening. And smack dab in the middle, he's hanging Bad Man Harper. It'll be quite a show."

"Hanging!" I whispered. I thought my knees were going to buckle.

35

"Of course, he could just slip that noose like he slipped that jail," said Skinhead. "It would ruin the show, but. . . ."

I choked back my tears. "You just can't leave us out here, Mr. Skinhead, you can't. Please don't take the balloon. I've got to get to my pa."

Skinhead drew out a dusty handkerchief and began polishing his skull.

"It would be the gentlemanly thing to do," said Weatherby.

"Well, I don't know," said Skinhead.

"Please, sir," I begged.

"As a tribute to Bad Man Harper," said Weatherby.

Skinhead blew his nose on the handkerchief and returned it to his pocket.

"All right, for the Bad Man," he said. He turned to his gang and shouted, "Boys, let's ride."

A loud groan went up from the outlaws. They had clearly been looking forward to putting a new wrinkle in their robberies.

"Mount up!" ordered Skinhead. He swung onto his horse. "Good luck, young Harper. You tell the Bad Man that Skinhead says hello." Before I could reply, the gang were whipping their horses toward the hills, raising a chorus of whoops and a cloud of choking dust.

I stared at Dr. Weatherby through the settling dust.

"The Fourth of July," I muttered.

"Just one week away," said Weatherby.

Chapter Seven

WASHOE ZEPHYR

We were soon aloft and drifting north on a wind that was barely a whisper. Virginia City still lay nearly seventy-five miles to the north, and our progress seemed painfully slow. I couldn't forget for a minute that there was a gallows waiting for my father.

From time to time Weatherby would try to cheer me with one of his yarns, but there was no shaking the gloom from my mind.

Late in the afternoon the sun dropped behind the Sierras. Before long, night crept over our balloon. As the stars came out one by one, the temperature dropped, and so did the balloon.

"If we get any lower, a cactus will spear us. We'll have to drop anchor," said Weatherby.

"It seems a shame to waste the wind," I said. "I'll gladly stand watch."

"Sorry, lad, but night flying is dangerous at best,"

said Weatherby. "Why, I remember one evening near Bodie when me and the ship. . . ."

All at once the wind stopped and an eerie, deathly quiet fell over us like a sudden chill. The wind hadn't withered away. It seemed to have been snatched away. For a moment we hung suspended in the silence. And then, with all the suddenness of a train breaking from a tunnel, the silence exploded into an incredible scream.

Weatherby dove for the bottom of the basket. I felt his hand grab me by the shoulder and pull me down. "Zephyr!" he cried. We were swallowed up in a whirlwind of choking dust and sand.

"Hold on," screamed Weatherby. And hold on I did. I dug my fingers into the wicker floor. Bottles spun about me like drunken tenpins.

The balloon was like a feather in a hurricane. Suddenly we'd be shot up hundreds of feet, and then, just as suddenly, we'd be plunged toward the rocky desert. When my stomach wasn't leaping up and down, it was turning cartwheels. I was so busy feeling sick, I didn't have time to be scared.

At one point a sudden gust of wind blew out the fire beneath the balloon in a shower of sparks and coals. There was nothing to keep us airborne but the wind. We were carried along for what felt like hours but could have been only minutes. We were battered, stung, choked, and pounded. The lines from the basket cracked like bullwhips, and the canvas snapped back and forth like laundry in the wind. I expected to die at any and every moment.

But then, as suddenly as it had all begun, the whirling stopped, the noise vanished, and we dropped toward the desert floor. We smashed into the sands with a jolt I thought would shorten me by two feet. As the dust settled, the doctor and I carefully untangled ourselves and stood up.

The desert was dark. The moon had yet to rise.

"Quite a blow, yes, quite a blow," said Weatherby, looking up at the balloon. "But it looks like most of our goods survived."

I hung onto the lip of the basket and peered out into the black. Weatherby gathered some coals and restarted the fire.

"Where are we?" I asked.

"The Washoe desert, I suspect," said Weatherby.

"Are we lost?"

"Only temporarily," said Weatherby. He leaned out over the basket and squinted up into the sky. "Don't worry, Jebidiah. We'll get our bearings from the stars."

My spirits rose. "You know the stars?" I asked hopefully.

"Know them?" Weatherby said with a laugh. "Why, I wouldn't be allowed to operate this airship without a knowledge of the heavens. Look up there. That's Pegasus, the winged horse, the prettiest sight in the sky."

I followed Weatherby's outstretched hand, but I couldn't make out anything that looked like a horse, winged or otherwise.

"Does Pegasus tell us where we are?" I asked.

"No, no," he said. "Antares should tell us that. She should be directly overhead."

"But shouldn't we try to find the North Star?" I asked. "My pa always told me to use it as a guide if I ever got lost."

"The North Star?" he asked.

"Yes," I said. "Haven't you heard of it?"

"Yes, of course," he said quickly. "She's right opposite the South Star, I believe."

"The South Star?" I said.

"Jebidiah," he said, patting me on the back, "don't you worry. I'll do the navigating."

The bag filled with hot air and the balloon slowly began to rise. However, she had suffered a number of small holes and couldn't seem to climb more than a few feet above the sand. All the while, Weatherby leaned out and gazed up at the stars. It was hard for me to imagine following something that sat directly over our heads. I hoped Weatherby knew what he was talking about.

After an hour or so, Weatherby mumbled something about Pisces the Fish, then said aloud, "I do believe that zephyr did us a favor. That little evening breeze has nudged us almost fifty miles closer to our destination."

"Then we're almost there!" I said excitedly.

"We're practically on top of her," said Weatherby. "In a few hours we'll find the sun rising to our right and Virginia City coming up dead ahead. You can rest easy, Jeb. We're close enough to stroll into town."

My joy at hearing this news lasted only until sunrise. When the sun came up it was to our left, instead of to our right as Weatherby had predicted. Worse yet, we were above a trackless desert that seemed to stretch on forever in all directions. As far as I could see, there was nothing but bent and twisted cactus and huge piles of black volcanic rock. There were no Sierras. There was no Virginia City. There was nothing out in that desert but the sun, the sand, and our battered and dying balloon.

Chapter Eight

BART AND FESTUS, AGAIN

By mid-morning the balloon could no longer lift us into the air. We climbed out, and I helped Weatherby haul the Ship of Health up onto a fifty-foot-high pile of black, pitted rocks. If it hadn't been for the thin web of wires inside the balloon, the whole airship would have collapsed into a heap. Nevertheless, she was dead in the desert. And I feared that, before long, we would be, too.

"No need to worry," said Weatherby cheerfully. "Someone's bound to come by and see the balloon. Prospectors are scratching about Nevada like chicks in a barnyard. I wager we'll be rescued by nightfall."

I gave him a dubious look. The place was as empty as a hole. Not a prospector was in sight. Nor, I thought, the prospect of one. I wasn't going to spend the next few days, or weeks, frying atop those rocks. Not with my father bound for the gallows.

"You can stay here, sir. But I'm going to walk to Virginia City."

"Virginia City? Which way might that be?" asked Weatherby. "In case it hasn't come to your attention, Jebidiah, we're lost."

"We've got to try something," I said.

Weatherby leaned back against a boulder and tipped his top hat over his eyes. "We're doing all we can," he said. "We're signaling. Relax. Enjoy the view."

I peered out across the desert. Blast! Weatherby was right. If I stomped off in the wrong direction, I'd end up snakebit and sunfried. I'd be of no use to Pa dead.

"Anyway," added Weatherby, "walking is out of the question. We need to conserve our strength. We've used up most of our water by now. We're down to half a bottle."

For the next two days we scoured the horizon for signs of life. And we baked. It felt like a million degrees up on those rocks. A cool breeze was rarer than a July snow, and so was a patch of shade.

Though we rationed the water, it was soon gone. My lips cracked, and my mouth went dry as dust. The only other liquid in the balloon was Weatherby's cure, but it was so shot with salt and tarantula juice it was useless.

By nightfall on the second day, we were near delirious with thirst.

"I'm sorry, Jeb," said Weatherby. "Maybe we should have tried to hike out."

"I'll never see my pa again," I said softly.

That night I dreamed that Pa and I were swimming in a mountain lake filled with sparkling water. We splashed each other. We laughed, and we drank the cold mountain water till it came out of our ears.

I was roused from this watery paradise by a pistol shot.

"You there, atop those rocks! Get down here!"

It was dawn. I shook the sleep from my head and tried to focus my eyes.

"Rise up!"

I peered down the hillside. Two men on horseback were eyeing us from below. A fat giant of a man with long, stringy hair was waving a pistol in the air. His partner was a squat, barrel-chested fellow in a dusty derby hat. My first thought was that they were desert desperadoes, no doubt cut from the same mold as Skinhead Dickerson and his boys. My second thought had to do with the canteen strapped to the fat man's horse. Worse than anything, I wanted a drink. So did Weatherby.

"Are we glad to see you," he shouted. "We haven't had a drop of water in nearly a day. You boys arrived just in time."

The fat man fired at our feet. "I said move!" he yelled.

We moved. I didn't like the thought of getting closer to that gun, but, heaven knows, I was thirsty.

As I made my way down the rocks, I studied the fat man. I'd seen that puffy face and heard that scratchy voice before. By the time I stepped off the rocks, I had him placed. He was Bart Means. At least, that's what he had called himself the night we'd met on the road. The night Orville Means had died. The doctor who'd accompanied him that night, the one called Festus, was sitting alongside Fat Bart. Since I'd seen him last, he'd sprouted a beard and exchanged his boots for moccasins. Long strips of leather, like a cat-o'-nine-tails, hung from his belt.

The fat man looked us over from his lofty perch and said, "We've been expecting you. What took you so long?"

"Expecting us?" said Weatherby. "Do you think we came to this awful place on purpose? Mister, we're lost."

"Lost? You two ain't lost," snorted Festus.

"Can we argue that later?" I said. "If you don't mind, I'd like a drink of water."

"Our water ain't for claim jumpers," said Bart. "The way I see it, you two have been trying to get at our Massacree Mine. Around these parts claim jumpers are shot. That's miner's law."

"Our business is in Virginia City, not here," said Weatherby. "All we ask is some water and a few directions, and we'll be on our way."

"Don't try to flumdoodle me," said Bart, leveling the pistol at Weatherby. "I aim to find out what you and young Harper are doing out here."

"Young Harper!" exclaimed Weatherby in surprise. "How do you know Jebidiah?"

46

"Why, we're old friends," said Bart. "Ain't we, boy?"

"Not friends, but we've met," I said. "These are the two men I told you about. The ones who were after that map to the Massacree Mine."

"The same map that must have led you here," said Bart. "Or have you been in Virginia City with your pa?"

"No, sir," I said. "But I'm trying to get to him. I aim to set him free."

Bart glanced over at Festus then back to me. "Then you haven't talked to your pa?"

"Not for months," I said.

"That's too bad," said Bart, lowering his pistol. "He would have told you all about us. We're partners. He gave us directions to the Massacree in return for half the gold. He wants you to have it after he's gone. He thinks a lot of you, Jeb."

I did wonder how they'd managed to find the Massacree. But sharing out his gold with those two didn't seem like something my pa would do.

"Luckily Dead-Eye Grady, the sheriff, is an old friend of ours. We rode together in Missouri," said Bart. "He was the one let us talk to your father."

"If we could have some water and directions, I'd be appreciative," I said. "I need to get to Virginia City."

"Now, don't be in such a hurry," said Bart. "I didn't tell you all this for nothing. The fact of the matter is that we could use a couple of skinny fellows like yourselves to help us at the mine. And, since half the gold is yours, Jeb, I thought you'd be glad to volunteer."

"I'm sorry," I said. "My pa is in a lot of trouble."

"All you have to do is work for us for a day, just till the yellow turns up. Then I'll take you and your friend into Virginia City. I'll even put in a good word about your pa with Dead-Eye," said Bart.

"I can't," I said. "My pa is due to be hung on the fourth, in three days."

Suddenly Bart's pistol came back up. This time it was pointed at me.

"I'm boss man out here," he said. "And I say you stay. Dr. Pangborn and I need your help."

Pangborn! The fact that I was staring into a loaded pistol suddenly seemed unimportant. Why, Festus Pangborn was the name of the man my pa was supposed to have murdered! I was looking either at a ghost or at the men who had framed my pa. No doubt they'd done it to find out the location of the Massacree.

I was madder than a hornet, but I tried not to let on. The less they thought I knew, the better. Besides, they had the water.

"Looks like we don't have much choice," I said.

"You said we only have to work for one day," said Weatherby.

"Not a second longer," said Bart.

"That a promise?" I asked.

"A promise," he said.

His word was worthless, but I was desperate.

"All right," I said.

"Fine," said Bart.

"Water," said I.

49

Bart gave me a toothy grin and threw me his canteen. I caught it in midair, yanked off the top, and
drank deeply. It tasted so good I almost cried. When
I was done, I passed the canteen to Weatherby.

"Let's go," said Bart. "It's not far."

Weatherby returned the canteen to me and I drank
again.

"I won't be wanting to leave my balloon here," said
Weatherby. "I wouldn't care to see it snatched away
by a zephyr."

Bart and Festus exchanged a quick glance. "It might
not be a bad idea to get that thing out of sight," said
Festus.

"All right, but step lively. There's work to be done,"
said Bart.

Weatherby lit the fire beneath the balloon. It rose
a foot or two, and he dragged it down the hillside. I
took up a rope, and we led it out across the sands. I
wondered where the mine was. I'd been scanning the
desert for days and hadn't noticed the slightest sign of
a mine. I reasoned the mystery would be solved soon
enough.

Chapter Nine

INTO THE MASSACREE MINE

We tramped along beneath a boiling sun. Bart, astride a coal-black horse with a white-tipped tail, led the way. We followed with the balloon, and Festus brought up the rear. As we walked, I told Weatherby my suspicions.

"I thought I'd heard the name Pangborn before," said Weatherby. "So you think they framed your pa?"

"Pa never would have told anyone about the Massacree," I said. "They must have forced it out of him in jail. It sounds to me like they're in cahoots with that Grady fellow who's the sheriff."

"They're lower than snakes, those two," said Weatherby.

"What do you think they'll do to us?" I asked.

"Don't worry about that," said Weatherby. "Start thinking about what we can do to get away from them."

After an hour's walk we mounted a low, circular ridge of rock and sand. Bart shouted us to a halt.

"There she is," he crowed. "The richest lode in all of Washoe."

When Weatherby and I came alongside him, we discovered that we were standing on the rim of a large volcanic crater. From one end to the other, it looked to be nearly half a mile across. Far below, the floor of the crater was pocked with scores of small round holes. Clouds of steam were squirting up from some of the holes, as if the volcano were fixing to erupt.

The place reminded me of Reverend Pritchett's description of the dark land of Hades.

"Great snakes alive!" shouted Weatherby, pointing down into the crater. "Is that what I think it is, lying on those boulders?"

I followed Weatherby's hand and then nearly shouted myself. It was a human skeleton!

"What is this place?" I gasped.

"You didn't think this place was named the Massacree because there'd been a picnic here, did you?" said Bart. "Twelve men died in this crater. Most of them were buried under a landslide. But the fella you're looking at must have been shot after the rocks came down. He's good company. Festus and I have kinda taken a liking to him."

I shuddered. "Who killed them?"

"The O'Sullivan gang," said Bart. "They massacreed twelve men down there. They would have killed thirteen, but one escaped."

"Who were the ones that got killed?" I asked.

"Easterners," said Bart. "They'd made a fortune in

52

the gold fields and were on their way back East. They were camped here when Casey O'Sullivan and his boys found them. The gang started a landslide that buried most of them. The others weren't about to let those bushwhackers have their gold, and so they tossed it in a hole, all thirty sacks of it, and covered it over with rocks. Not long afterward, the gang finished them off."

"But you said one escaped," said Weatherby.

"One did. Orville Means was his name," said Bart. "He squirreled himself away in the rocks and laid low till the O'Sullivans cleared out. A month later he was back in California rustling up the supplies he needed to fish out the gold."

"How do you know all this?" asked Weatherby.

"We met Means in a saloon outside of Sacramento," said Festus. "He had a weakness for strong drink, and he got to talking. I wouldn't say he invited us along, but he didn't exactly disinvite us, either."

"So you followed him," I said.

"We were heading in the same direction, if that's what you mean," said Festus.

"So what did you do after Means died?" I asked.

"Well," said Festus. "We . . ."

"Pangborn, that's enough of your yapping," said Bart suddenly. "There's work to be done."

"But, Bart, I . . ."

"Shut up!" said the fat man. "Let's go."

Bart eased his horse over the rim, and we began to follow him down a steep, sandy trail toward the crater floor.

53

"Mind your step," he barked. "These rocks are looser than bad teeth. Unless you want to bury us all, don't so much as spit on one of those stones."

Burying Bart would have been fine with me. Though Festus hadn't said so, I was certain those two had followed my pa from Placerville. By the time he got to Virginia City, Pa probably realized he was being tailed and tried to shake them. That's when they must have gotten together with their sheriff friend, Grady, and arranged to have my father thrown in jail for murder. I hoped they hadn't hurt him in jail, but they sure had done something to get him to talk. I wasn't positive that was the way things had happened, but it made sense.

When we reached the floor of the crater, Weatherby snuffed out the charcoal fire and let the ship settle into a rocky corner. I glanced around. The crater walls rose steeply on all sides. It reminded me of a picture I had once seen of the Roman Colosseum, the place where they used to feed people to lions.

"My, my," clucked Bart, climbing down off his horse. "I don't think we could have found better miners in all of creation. I declare, Dr. Festus, these two are skinnier than sticks."

"I'm afraid you'll be disappointed," said Dr. Weatherby, dusting off his top hat. "My calling is doctoring, not mining."

Festus spat into the dust. "Doctoring! Why, you're no more a doctor than that nag I rode in on. No real doctor would travel about in a painted flying machine."

"And just what manner of medicine do *you* practice, doctor?" asked Weatherby.

Festus stepped forward till he was toe to toe with Weatherby.

"I practice healing medicine, and I'm proud of it," he said. "I am the purveyor of Pangborn's Magic Swamp Root Elixir, the greatest cure in the history of medicine. It'll put hair on a bald man, cure the corns on his feet, and tidy up everything in between as well. And, unlike that poison you're peddling, it works."

"Works! Works on what, lizards?" said Dr. Weatherby. "No offense, sir, but I sell my medicine to people, and out here there seems to be a frightful scarcity of human folks. But don't get me wrong, I don't mean to slight lizard-doctoring. Treating slimy creatures is a noble profession, I'm sure."

Festus Pangborn's eyes glowed like coals. In another moment they would have come to blows if Bart had not suddenly stepped between them.

"You can settle this later," said Bart. "We've gold to fetch. Festus, scare up some rope."

"You're just lucky you're so skinny," said Festus, heading for a pile of scrap wood and rusting cans. "If you fellows were fat, you'd still be frying out in that desert."

I couldn't understand why being skinny made me so valuable. The only other person who'd ever noticed my bony body was my pa, and he was always trying to fatten me up.

Bart led us over to one of the deep holes that pocked the crater floor.

"This is the money pit," he said, pointing down the narrow shaft. "There's a right smart bit of rock and sand down there on top of the gold. You're going to haul it out."

I peered down into the black hole. It looked bottomless.

"I don't believe I'll be climbing in there," I said. "Gold or no, it don't look safe."

"Do as I say, Jeb," ordered Bart.

"No, sir," I said.

Suddenly Bart pulled his pistol out of his belt. "You work for me now, boy. And I aim to have that gold. Is that clear?"

I glared back at him but didn't reply.

"You can't force the lad into that hole," said Weatherby.

Bart waved the gun at Weatherby. "Shut your mouth," he said. "Festus, hurry up with that rope."

Festus reappeared with two long ropes. One he attached to a small wooden bucket, which he lowered into the shaft. Then, while Bart covered me with his pistol, Festus wound the second rope around my ankles and tied a huge knot.

"What's this for?" I asked anxiously. "What are you doing?"

Festus replied by wrapping his arms around my waist and spinning me upside down. I found myself looking squarely into the hole.

"Let me go!"

And he did. Suddenly I was being lowered away. I kicked and squirmed but couldn't keep from slipping deeper into the darkness. At last I was jerked to a halt. Through the gloom I made out the bucket resting atop a pile of sand and rock.

"Fill up that bucket!" I heard Bart shout.

In due time, I thought. He'd find me the slowest, laziest miner in all of Washoe. I threw a handful of sand into the bucket while I bobbled about like a worm on a hook. There was gold somewhere beneath me, but I didn't fancy hauling it up for Fat Bart.

The voice of Festus Pangborn came rattling down the shaft. "How's your head feeling?"

I thought my eyes were going to pop. I imagined my face was already tomato red and hurrying toward purple. But I didn't favor him with a reply.

I scooped some sand and rock into the bucket and shouted for them to haul me up. I came shooting up to the surface like a hooked fish. They stood me on my feet and drained some of the blood from my skull.

"If you don't mind," I said, "I'd just as soon not go down there again." The last of these words was spoken as Bart lifted me off the ground, spun me upside down, and started me back down the shaft.

Chapter Ten

THE MAGIC SWAMP ROOT ELIXIR

I spent the next hour or so being thrown into and fished out of the Massacree Mine. When Bart and Festus decided I had had enough, I was relieved by Dr. Weatherby, who had the sad misfortune of being nearly as thin as I was.

I sat nearby and watched for a chance to take Bart and Festus by surprise. I reasoned that if I could somehow take them unawares, I could bean their thick skulls with a Massacree stone. But the opportunity never seemed to come up. There was always an eye on me, and sometimes a gun as well.

As the morning wore on, the temperature soared. There were times when the ground felt so hot I thought the volcano beneath us was going to explode. Fat Bart was lathered in sweat, but he wouldn't leave that shaft. His mind burned with greed. He pawed through every bucket of rock that came up. And when he didn't find any nuggets, he'd curse the sand, spit on the stones, and send us back down for more.

Finally, a little after midday, we stopped for lunch of hard bread and cold beans, leftovers from some earlier meal. As I sat and ate, I looked around the Massacree Mine. The bushwhacked miners had left behind a storehouse of goods. I saw tools, sacks of beans and rice, barrels of water, even a case of dynamite. I made a mental note of the dynamite. It could come in handy, though it wouldn't be much use in the crater. One stick would be enough to bring the walls crashing down on all of us.

I had hardly finished my meal when Bart ordered everyone back to work.

"Let's scare up that yellow," he said.

"Can't we wait till the sun gets a little lower?" I asked. "It's hotter'n blazes in that shaft."

"The sooner we have the gold, the sooner you'll be free," said Bart. "Find that gold, and I promise you a nice reward."

I didn't doubt that the reward—most likely, a one-way trip into the shaft.

All that afternoon, Weatherby and I hauled rocks. I was yanked up and down that shaft so many times I nearly wore clean through my britches. We must have dug down nearly ten feet. I was beginning to wonder whether we weren't looking in the wrong hole, and whether there was any gold there at all.

Though we were doing all the work, Bart was the

one that sweated. Any other man would have sought out a scrap of shade. But not Bart. He had the worst case of gold fever I'd ever seen. He was a madman.

Along about mid-afternoon my hand grabbed hold of something very unlike a rock. In the dim light I couldn't see a thing, but my fingers told me all I needed to know. I'd struck leather! I groped about till I'd made out the lumpy shape of a sack. No doubt there were twenty-nine others beneath it. I dug into the rotting leather and came up with a big nugget, which I grasped tightly in my hand.

I didn't dare let Bart know I'd found the treasure. Sending up those nuggets would be like signing a death warrant for me and Weatherby. Of that I was certain.

"Confound you, boy! What's taking so long?" It was the voice of the fat man.

I scraped up the few remaining rocks and tossed them in the bucket.

"I'm done! Haul away!"

"Nothing yet?" said Bart, when I was back on top.

"No, sir," I said, slipping the nugget into my pocket while Bart dumped out the bucket.

"Blast!" he cursed, peering into the murky shaft. "Blast if I hadn't just smelled gold."

He spat angrily into the dust and pounded off toward where we'd eaten earlier. He was probably headed for the canteen. But he never made it.

The sun had finally gotten to fat Bart. All day long it had pounded him with fists of fire. And now it had him reeling. He staggered toward the canteen, weaving like a drunk. At last, like a redwood falling under the ax, he fainted dead away, rising a cloud of dust as he slapped into the ground.

"Fire and blazes!" exclaimed Festus. "Bart's been seized with the dropsy!"

Festus hurried to his partner's side and took his pulse.

"It's just as I thought, dropsy," he said. "The only thing that can save him now is Pangborn's Magic Swamp Root Elixir."

He stood up and waved his pistol in our direction. "You two sit tight."

He scurried off toward a pile of splintered boxes.

"The man's clearly suffering from apoplexy, not dropsy," said Weatherby. "Just look how red his face is."

To me it appeared he had sunstroke, but I didn't think either doctor wanted my opinion.

"I could bring him around in a second with a shot of the Heavenly Remedy, but you won't find me lifting a finger to help that blubber-faced scoundrel," said Weatherby. "He can bake out here forever as far as I'm concerned. Let his friend poison him with that lizard potion. It's nothing but whiskey anyway."

Whiskey! The word kicked a full-blown idea into my head.

"Dr. Weatherby," I said. "Maybe we should help Bart."

"What?" said Weatherby.

"I've got a plan," I said.

My idea for escape was surprisingly simple. As I whispered it to Weatherby, he nodded solemnly. Then, when I was done, his face lit up in a smile and he gave me a slap on the back. "My boy, you're a genius. We're as good as gone."

Pangborn returned with a tall brown bottle, which he uncorked and pressed to Bart's lips. I could smell the whiskey from where I sat, but I guess whiskey was what the fat man needed, because in a few minutes I saw Bart's eyes flutter open.

"Will you look at that, another cure for the Magic Elixir," boasted Festus, and to toast the occasion, he took a swig of his own medicine.

Bart rubbed his head and stared up into Pangborn's face. "What happened?" he mumbled.

"You were dropsy-seized. If it hadn't been for the Magic Elixir, you'd have been a goner," said Festus.

"Hold on. You're not out of the woods yet," said Weatherby, rolling to his feet and walking toward Bart and Festus. "You don't have dropsy, you've got apoplexy. You could have another stroke at any minute. Next one's likely to be fatal."

"Bunkum!" said Festus.

"And you call yourself a doctor," said Weatherby with disgust. "Just look at his red face, Pangborn. That's apoplexy. This man's near death."

"Hogwash!" snorted Festus.

"Festus, you could go any moment, too," said

Weatherby, pointing a finger at Dr. Pangborn. "You two have been out in this sun so long your bodies are salt-starved. That's apoplexy."

"It is?" said Bart.

"Why, just look at his eyes, Bart. See how puffy they are," said Weatherby.

Bart sat up and studied Pangborn's face. "His eyes do seem kinda blown up," he said. "You say that's a sign?"

"As sure as I'm standing here."

Bart rubbed the sweat from his cheek and looked at his damp hand.

"Is there a cure?" he asked in an unsteady voice.

"That's where you're in luck," said Weatherby. "The Heavenly Remedy is specially salt-brewed just for apoplexy. Give me the word, and I'll break it out."

"Keep that poison to yourself," said Festus. "If it's apoplexy we've got, then it's my elixir that's called for."

Weatherby took off his hat and bent down toward Bart. "Listen," he said. "Why take a chance? Lengthen out the odds. Take both cures. It can't hurt."

Bart didn't hesitate to agree. "Weatherby, fetch up that remedy of yours."

Within minutes Bart and Festus were swigging down bottles of apoplexy medicine. For every dose of Heavenly Remedy that was belted down, Festus insisted they also drink a pint of elixir. I sat nearby, rubbing my boots with a rag and watching the party.

My plan was working perfectly. They drank till they

were stewed, and they continued straight on till they were pickled.

Near sundown Festus finally passed out, but Bart wouldn't go down. And the drunker he got, the more dangerous he became. Suddenly he had his gun out and was pointing it at Weatherby.

"More of that cure," he growled, fighting to keep his balance. "Make it quick, or I'll plug you."

He let off a round at Weatherby, but fortunately, he missed. Before he could fire again, I tried to distract him. "Bart, be careful."

He spun around to face me. Something about me must have struck him as funny, for he started to smile, but just as quickly his expression changed to one of surprise. "Jebidiah," he said, with a wave of the pistol. "Come here."

Suddenly he didn't sound drunk. "What do you want, more medicine?" I asked, walking slowly toward him.

"It ain't medicine I'm after, Jebidiah Harper. It's you," he snarled, seizing me suddenly by the arm. "It's you, you sniveling cheat."

"Cheat?" I said.

"Wanted it all for yourself, did you? Filled your pockets with Bart's gold, I see."

I glanced down and was immediately horrified. The scraping up and down the shaft had worn a hole in my pocket. Peeking through the gap, shining like a beacon, was my gold nugget.

"By the blazes! It's gold!" he shouted.

With his free hand he tried to rip away my pocket.

Then, suddenly, there was a loud crack! and he fell in a heap at my feet. Behind him stood Dr. Weatherby with a bottle of Heavenly Remedy.

"Didn't I say there wasn't a thing my cure couldn't fix?" said the doctor, laughing.

"You have my thanks," I said.

Weatherby walked over and untied the two horses. "Care to join me, Jebidiah? I'm thinking of heading for Virginia City."

"Yes," I said, smiling. "I'm feeling in a traveling mood."

I boosted myself aboard Festus's brown steed, and Weatherby climbed atop Bart's horse, the coal-black nag with the white-tipped tail.

We trotted past the sleeping men and mounted the trail that zigzagged up the crater wall. I hung back a few paces to avoid the tumbling rocks. We paused at the top and then turned right to what I hoped was Virginia City.

It was the second of July. I had two days left to save my father's life.

Chapter Eleven

MR. DEAD-EYE GRADY

Night came, and with it, enough of a moon to light our way into the rocky desert. We picked up a rough trail and followed it west.

"Do you reckon we're heading right?" I asked.

"A trail in these parts is rarer than a three-dollar bill. It's got to lead somewhere important. Around here that has to mean Virginia City," said Weatherby.

We rode for long stretches in silence. But once, sometime near dawn, Weatherby said, "I'm sure you and your father will soon be riding for California, but— well, if anything happens, then I'd like you to consider staying on with me. I'd be proud to have you as a son."

I felt a lump growing in my throat. I liked Weatherby, but I hoped nothing would happen to my pa. "Thank you, sir," I said.

"I'd be mighty proud," he repeated.

67

When at last the sky began to lighten, I discovered that we were riding into a chain of low, scrub-covered hills.

"The Washoe Mountains," said Weatherby. "I'd be willing to wager that Virginia City's dead ahead."

We spurred our horses on. We wound our way up into the hills. In the distance a thin column of dust was rising.

"Looks like someone's coming our way," said Weatherby. "He's in a hurry, too."

The rider came charging through the hills like a Washoe Zephyr. In short order he had drawn alongside us and pulled his horse to a halt.

When the dust had settled, I made out a big-nosed man with a stubbly beard and a patch over one eye.

"Where you folks headed?" he inquired.

"Virginia City," said Weatherby. "We'd be obliged if you could tell us whether we're pointed the right way."

"She's not far," he said. He eyed Weatherby's horse. "That's a pretty filly you have there."

"Thank you, sir," said the doctor. "I see you appreciate good horseflesh."

The one-eyed man spat into the dust. "Don't see many horses marked like that, all black with a white tail."

"Believe me, it's nothing special," said Weatherby. "There's a whole heap of them where we come from."

The stranger smiled. "And just where might that be? The Massacree Mine?"

I almost fell off my horse! Did every rider in Nevada know about the mine?

But if Weatherby was surprised, he didn't show it. "Massacree? Name doesn't ring a bell. It near here?"

"I'm surprised you ain't familiar with it. The trail you're on leads directly there."

"We must have passed it in the night," said Weatherby. "Now, if you'll excuse us, we'll be on our way."

Weatherby slapped the horse and started forward. He hadn't taken more than a step when the stranger suddenly drew a pistol.

"Enough of this humbuggery. Where'd you get that horse?"

When Weatherby refused to answer, he shifted the pistol from the doctor to me.

"If I don't have an answer in ten seconds, I aim to lighten the load on this nag's back," he said. "One, two . . ."

Weatherby and I exchanged a worried glance.

"Six, seven, eight . . ."

"Put away the gun," sighed Weatherby. "I'll tell you what you want to know."

The one-eyed man smiled, but then his grin became a scowl.

"Boy! Where did you get that walking leather?"

"What?"

"Those boots. Where did they come from?"

The stranger was an outlaw if I'd ever seen one. My boots had saved us once from desert desperadoes. I gambled they'd rescue us again.

69

"Haven't you heard of Bad Man Harper? He's my pa," I said proudly.

The one-eyed man smiled again. "I thought you might be Harper kin. Sure, I've heard of your pa, and he's heard of me, too. Yes, sir, I bet your daddy never will forget old Dead-Eye Grady."

I felt as if I'd been struck by lightning. "Why, you're the man that jailed my pa. You're the sheriff!"

"I *was* the sheriff," he said, anxiously looking over his shoulder. "The good folks of Virginia City and I have just recently parted ways."

"You have my sympathy," said Weatherby.

"I was hoping that my friends out at the Massacree would have hunted up enough gold so that Dead-Eye wouldn't have to work any more, but I see things have not been going well. Why don't we all just mosey on out there? I'm certain my friends want their horses back. Let's ride!"

And so we rode. Away from Virginia City, and Pa. Back into the desert. Back to Bart and Festus, and back to thirty sacks of deadly Massacree gold.

Chapter Twelve

WORK, OR DIE

I was desperately tired. We hadn't slept in more than a day, but Dead-Eye kept us on the move. We paused but once, to drink from a foul Washoe spring and to eat from a loaf of stale bread that Grady took out of his pack.

"Is my father going to be all right?" I asked.

"He's going to hang," said Grady.

I wanted to know more, but Grady wouldn't talk. He seemed lost in his own dark thoughts, and he didn't speak again except to deliver orders and commands.

At sunset, when the Massacree Mine finally hove into view, I was swept with a feeling of darkest dread. I pulled the nugget out of my pocket and let it drop near the trail. I wasn't about to let Bart have it.

At the lip of the crater Dead-Eye fired off a round.

The report echoed from the crater walls and touched off a score of small landslides.

"Anybody home?" he shouted.

Through the gloomy dusk I saw Bart and Festus come storming out from behind a boulder.

"What are you aiming to do, bury us alive?" screamed Bart. "Fire and blazes, Dead-Eye, you gone crazy?"

We eased our way into the crater.

"Mind who you call crazy," said Dead-Eye. "I seem to be the one with your horses." He paused and looked around the darkened crater. "Things look about the same as when I was here two months ago. You found the gold yet?"

"Not yet, but it's practically in our pockets," said Bart. "Hop down and I'll explain everything. Festus, tie up those two."

We dismounted, and Festus showed us over to a post where the horses had once been tethered. He took the leather thongs that hung from his belt and used them to tie our hands behind the post.

"Bart spent most of the morning with a hook and a line trying to fish up those sacks," he said, cinching down the leather. "He aims to have your hides. Me too."

"He can have what he wants," I said. "But I won't bring up that gold."

Darkness came quickly. Festus built a fire and soon, out of the flickering light, Bart came waddling toward us. He squatted down and fixed me with a cold eye.

"If there was more light, I'd have you at work right

now," he said. "But I suppose the gold will keep. You'll finish your work in the morning."

I returned his gaze as best I could. "I reckon you're wrong. You can hang me by my feet or even by my neck, if that's more to your liking, but I won't bring up the gold. Why should I? You're going to kill us anyway."

"Don't be contrary, boy. If you cooperate, you'll be free to go. You have my word on that."

I didn't consider his word worth beans. "I won't do it."

Bart spat angrily into the sand and rose to his feet.

"You will work, or you and the doctor here will die with Apache bonnets wrapped around your skulls. You're forcing my hand. By jasper, if it comes down to a choice between you and the gold, I'll have to choose on the side of the shiny stuff."

He spat again, wheeled around, and strode away toward the fire. Out on the rocks, not ten feet away, I could make out the bleached bones of the bushwhacked miner. I wondered what an Apache bonnet was.

Chapter Thirteen
THE APACHE BONNET

Weatherby and I slept sitting up, back to back, our hands tied around the post. Just before dawn I awoke. It was the Fourth of July. Across the sands in Virginia City, my father was awaiting the hangman. I ached to see him one last time before he died, before I died, today.

Not long after daybreak the Massacree Mine began to come to life.

"Morning," said Weatherby.

"Morning," said I.

"Morning," said Bart. He'd come strolling up with a pot of water in one hand and two long leather thongs in the other.

"Ready to work?" he asked me.

"Not for you," I said.

"See this leather?" he said, dangling the thongs before my eyes. "This is an Apache bonnet. Indians invented it. You wet it down and wrap it around a man's skull. If you know your cowhide, then you'll know that leather shrinks when it dries. You can imagine what that does to your head."

It was something I could imagine all too well. A person's head would crack open like an overripe melon.

"You can put those things on me, but I won't go into your blasted mine," I said.

Bart dropped the thongs into the pot, let them soak, and then pulled the dripping leather out of the water.

"Don't you worry, Jeb," said Bart. "These are for Dr. Weatherby."

"Don't let him fool you into getting that gold," said Weatherby. "Once he has it, he'll kill us both."

"Last chance," said Bart, setting down the pot and walking around to Weatherby.

I held my tongue as Bart wrapped the thongs tightly around Weatherby's head, tucked in the ends, and wiped his hands on his pants.

"How do you like the bonnet?" he asked Weatherby.

"Quite comfortable. The wet leather is nice and cool," said Weatherby.

"You'll change your story when the sun peeks over those rocks," said Bart. "You're going to have a headache that nothing can cure, not even that pronto remedy of yours."

"Take that thing off," I said. "You got no right."

"The moment you go into that shaft, I'll peel off the bonnet," said Bart.

"Let those bags rot," I said.

"Then so will the doctor, my friend." And he turned and walked away.

An hour later the sun had crested the rocks and the leather had begun to dry. I could tell that Weatherby was in pain by the way he twisted against the post.

"How do you feel?" I asked.

"Couldn't be better," he said softly.

I kicked out in frustration and almost upset the pot of water Bart had left at my feet. It was the same water he had used to make the bonnet. By ginger! I thought, if leather shrank when it dried, then it had to expand when it was wetted. I hooked my foot around the pot and dragged it to the post. I shifted it back and forth with my body till I brought it alongside my wrists. I slipped my hands into the water and let the leather drink up the moisture.

"Dr. Weatherby!" I whispered. "I think I can get loose."

At once I began to work the damp leather back and forth. I wriggled and stretched and twisted. The bonds began to loosen. Then, all at once, I gave a mighty jerk and my hands pulled free.

"I did it!" I whispered excitedly. "I'll get the . . ."

"Gold is what you'll get," boomed the voice of Fat Bart. I whipped around and saw him hulking over Weatherby. I had been so busy I hadn't seen him sneaking up.

"You saved us the trouble of unhitching you. Ready to work?"

I was crushed. I had been so close.

"Your friend doesn't look well. You sure you won't reconsider?"

"Don't you mind about me," groaned Weatherby.

It pained me something awful to see that leather strangling his head. Tears came to my eyes. I bit my lip to choke them back.

"I hear it's something awful when the head splits open," said Bart.

"Please," I begged.

"It's not up to me, it's up to you, Jeb."

Weatherby moaned.

"Last chance," said Bart, starting to walk away.

I lowered my head. "Wait," I said. "I'll work."

Bart clapped his hands and gave me a grin. "Now you're talking sense."

He loosened the Apache bonnet and said, "No tricks, now. Next time the hat will stay on."

Bart jerked me to my feet and yelled for Festus.

"Rustle up the rope. We got ourselves a Massacree miner."

We came together at the money pit. Bart watched while Festus looped a noose around my ankles. The fat man rubbed his hands in expectation. His eyes were glazed over with greed.

Suddenly a voice rang out from the rim of the crater.

"Reach, all of you!"

Chapter Fourteen
FOURTH-OF-JULY FIREWORKS

I jerked around and saw two men on horseback up on the rim of the crater. The man who had shouted was sighting down the barrel of a silver rifle. The other one wore a red bandanna around his neck and a shapeless hat that all but hid his face. More bandits, I thought. Tarnation! There seemed to be more outlaws slithering about Nevada than rattlers.

"Grab a piece of the sky!" barked the gunman.

We reached for the heavens.

The strangers slowly eased their horses down the trail.

Dead-Eye had kept out of sight, and now I saw him drop between two rocks and draw his pistol. Perhaps the two gangs of outlaws would shoot it out and kill each other to the last man. I just hoped Weatherby and I would be able to stay clear of the fracas.

As the strangers drew closer, I saw the sun gleaming off of something on the rifleman's shirt. I blinked, and then blinked again. My heart leaped. It was the law!

Too late I remembered Dead-Eye Grady.

"Hold it right there," said Grady, rising from between the boulders. He'd been waiting for a chance to get a drop on the sheriff. And now he had it.

"Let go of that rifle, sheriff. Lay 'er down nice and easy-like," said Dead-Eye.

The sheriff let the rifle drop into the dust. Then he turned around and faced Dead-Eye. "I thought I'd find you out here, Dead-Eye. It looks like the citizens of Virginia City should have run you out of the territory, not just the town."

"I guess they should have, at that, Sheriff Hadley. Now, if you'll just slide off those horses, I won't be obliged to blow them out from under you."

The sheriff and his sidekick quickly dismounted.

Grady's words may have frightened the sheriff, but all they did to me was give me an idea. The idea was the case of dynamite I'd seen earlier. I'd known there'd be a time when a stick of that stuff would come in handy. Now was that time.

While everyone's eyes were on the sheriff, I undid the rope from around my ankles and edged over to the case of dynamite. I reached in and pulled out a single stick. My plan was to touch off a landslide, one big enough to cause some confusion, but not so big as to bury us all. I didn't know the odds, but it was clear that if I did nothing, we were all done for.

I looked to the rear of the mine and caught Weatherby's eye. He gave me a nod, and I heaved the stick onto the smoldering campfire. I held my breath. My heart pounded. Then the campfire exploded in a tremendous shower of sparks and fire. The noise boomed, and then it echoed off the crater walls. It was the Fourth of July at the Massacree Mine.

The blast lifted us off our feet. Smoke and dust filled the crater like a hot, stinging fog. I couldn't see, but it was easy enough to pinpoint the others by the coughing and cursing that soon filled the air. In the confusion I managed to scoop up the sheriff's rifle. I made out Dead-Eye Grady through the haze.

"Drop that gun!" I ordered.

He swung around to face me. "I'm going to drop you, kid," he said.

My finger twitched against the trigger. I was preparing to shoot, but instead I shouted, "Run!"

The blast had loosened one whole side of the crater. Boulders as big as houses were starting to dance down upon us.

Everyone went streaking to the far side of the crater, near where Weatherby was tied. The whole side of the hill seemed on the move. Boulders came roaring out of the smoke and dust. They crashed crazily into one another, splitting into a thousand pieces of sharp volcanic rock. Horses reared and whinnied. Men screamed and cursed. I tumbled over, fell down, and got up again.

And then, all at once, a giant boulder was bearing

down on me like a runaway train. I dove behind a rock. The boulder clipped the top off the rock and skipped by in a shower of stinging dust.

I didn't take my hands away from my eyes till I felt a tap on my shoulder. When I did, I found myself staring at a pair of boots. Fancy boots they were, with big red *H*'s cut into the sides. I rose up and looked the man in the face.

"Pa!" I yelled. And I leaped into my father's outstretched arms.

Chapter Fifteen

FAMILY

While the dust was settling and the rocks were coming to rest, Pa and I hugged each other till I thought our bones would crack. By ginger! I was alive, and so was my pa.

"I didn't know it was you with the sheriff," I said.

"I was surprised to see you, too, Jebidiah. But I did know you were in Nevada," he said.

"How'd you know that?" I asked.

"An old friend of yours told me. A cellmate of mine in Virginia City. Man by the name of Skinhead Dickerson," said Pa.

"Skinhead!" I said. "He must have been excited to meet you. He thought you were awful special for busting that jail."

"I didn't bust out of there, Jeb. Grady let me out."

"Why'd he do that?" I asked.

"We made a deal," said Pa. "I didn't want to hang for a murder I didn't commit. So, when Grady and Bart said they'd let me go if I told them where the Massacree gold was, I agreed. I wasn't gone but two days when Grady ran me down and put me back in jail. The jail-busting proved my guilt, said the folks in Virginia City."

"I thought sure they were going to hang you," I said.

"And they almost did. But two days ago a Dead-or-Alive poster for the Dead-Eye gang turned up in town. Everyone went crazy. They meant to have Grady's hide. Seems there's a sizable reward for his capture."

Through the dusty haze I could make out the sheriff rounding up the dazed members of the Dead-Eye gang.

"Hadley became the new sheriff," said Pa. "He knew I'd been framed, and so he let me go. Grady was gone by then, but I was sure I knew where he was going: the Massacree."

"There's not much left of it now," I said. "The gold is buried under a whole mountain of rock, and so is Dr. Weatherby's ship."

"Dr. Weatherby?" said Pa.

"Dr. Weatherby!" I exclaimed. In the excitement I had forgotten all about my friend.

I scurried over to the post and untied Weatherby.

"Are you all right?" I asked.

"I think I'll take a smaller hat from now on, but otherwise I'm fine," he said as he slowly got to his feet.

The doctor and I walked over to where the sheriff and my pa were tying up the Dead-Eye gang.

"Pa," I said. "I want you to meet my friend, Dr. Weatherby. He's the one that brought me here."

"You should be proud of this boy," said Weatherby. "He's something special."

"I know that," said Pa, shaking the doctor's hand. "And thank you for looking after him."

Weatherby looked around the crater. "Too bad about the gold," he said. "Looks like it's gone for good."

"The gold doesn't matter to me," I said. "I got my pa. I don't need any money."

"Does that mean you're not interested in the reward?" said the sheriff.

"Reward?"

"The reward for the capture of the Dead-Eye gang. It's a hefty sum."

"And it might be mine?"

"No mights about it," said the sheriff. "You're the one that corralled them."

"I want to split it with the doctor," I said. "He's going to need a new balloon to replace the one I just buried."

"I accept your generosity, but I think my flying days are over," said Weatherby. "It's time I settled down. From what I understand, Virginia City is full of disease. Sounds like the perfect place for me and the remedy to sink our roots."

"And what about us, Pa? Are we going back to Placerville?"

The sheriff put his hand on my father's shoulder. "Jake's not going back to California. He's staying with me at the Virginia City jail."

I was thunderstruck. "But Pa was framed. You can't take him back."

"You got me wrong," said Sheriff Hadley. "I want your pa at the jailhouse, but not as a prisoner. I've asked him to be my deputy. He's all but agreed to take the job."

Pa shook his head. "Not so fast, Hadley. It all depends on what Jebidiah wants to do."

"Speaking for myself, I hope you choose to stay," said Weatherby. "I've gotten used to your company."

"If you like, you could be the boy's uncle," said Pa. "He's never had one."

Suddenly Weatherby looked a little misty-eyed. "I'd like that very much," he said.

"And so would I," I said.

"So which is it, Jeb, Nevada or California?" said Pa.

"Well," I said, "in California they called me Orphan Jeb, but they won't call me that here in Nevada. I've got a family here now, a father and even an uncle."

"So, then, you want to stay," said Pa.

"Yes, sir," I said with a smile. "I think Nevada is going to suit me just fine."

Stephen Mooser was born in Fresno, CA, and holds degrees in motion pictures and journalism from UCLA. He has worked as a film director/photographer and as a reporter, and has hunted for pirate treasure in Panama and for outlaw gold in Utah.

Mr. Mooser, who has been writing since first grade, began his professional career in children's books with a 250-book reading series. He has since written ten trade books for young readers, and now devotes full time to free-lance writing. Mr. Mooser is president of the Society of Children's Book Writers. He and his wife have two children and currently reside in New York City.

Joyce Audy dos Santos received her art training at Massachusetts College of Art and the Harvard School of Design. She has illustrated several books for children, including *Henri and the Loup-Garou*, which she also wrote, and Barbara Costikyan's *Be Kind to Your Dog at Christmas*. She lives with her three children in Merrimac, Massachusetts.